VIRUS

Mary Chapman

Evans

For Freda, for friendship

Published by Evans Brothers Limited
2A Portman Mansions
Chiltern St
London W1U 6NR

© Mary Chapman 2007

First published in 2007

British Library Cataloguing in Publication Data
Chapman, Mary
   Virus. - (Shades)
   1. Young adult fiction
   I. Title
   823.9'2[J]

ISBN-13: 9780237532062

Series Editor: David Orme
Editor: Julia Moffatt
Designer: Rob Walster

Chapter One

'Time-to get-up!'

A high-pitched voice snapped instructions
at Penna. A green light flashed on the tiny
screen of her LOP – her Life Organisation
Programmer. It had been with her from birth,
welded to her wrist in the delivery room.
Her Sleeper moved into the upright
position, gently tipping her on to the floor.

'Time-to-shower!'

In the Wet-Room jets of water sprayed all over her from walls, floor and ceiling. Soapy foam squirted on to her hair and body, followed by more water. She stepped into the Dry-Room; gusts of warm air blew from ducts all around her.

'Time-to-dress!'

Penna tapped Workday 499 into the keypad on the front of the Clothing Cabinet in the Dressing-Room. Three drawers slid open, labelled: *Underwear*, *Outerwear*, *Footwear*. She knew from the contents that it was going to be a cold day.

Even before she'd finished dressing her LOP was issuing the next instruction.

'Time-to-input!'

In the Input-Room she activated the Body-State Monitor on her LOP, checked her body mass index, blood pressure, pulse

4

and heart rate, and then pressed the Input
Key. Codes for the three Recommended
Inputs for the day appeared on the screen.

At the Input-Cabinet she entered the code
for her first input. From the Dispensing-
Drawer she took a covered bowl containing
a mound of green jelly-like substance, thin
orange rectangles and a dollop of yellow
creamy stuff. She peeled the transparent
lid off the bowl, unclipped the spoon from
the side, and quickly ate the contents. Then
she threw the spoon and empty bowl into
the waste-chute.

'Time-to-output!'

As she left the Output-Room, Penna
clipped on her belt-pouch. She aimed her
Remote Control at the door, stepped out into
the corridor and straight on to the crowded
Verticalator. Swiftly it took her the thirty
floors down to the ground where she

transferred to the Horizontalator for the
second stage of her journey.

She got off at the Instruction Zone Exit
and hurried along the tunnel to the Middle
Arena.

'Time-to-return-to-Living-Unit!'

It was an automated voice message from
her LOP. But she'd only just arrived.

*'Time-to-return-to-Living-Unit! … return-to-
Living-Unit! … Time-to … Living-Unit! Time-
to-return…'*

Everybody's LOPs were also issuing
instructions. What was happening?

'…return-to-Living-Unit! … Unit … time…'

She looked around the Arena. The other
students appeared bewildered, still sitting,
staring at their screens. The noise from the
LOPS was increasing.

'All our LOPs have gone wrong. What's
going on?'

It was strange to hear another student's voice when normally they didn't talk to each other. They were tuned in to their LOPs all the time, and in the Instruction Zone they were entirely focused on their computer screens.

'Er, I don't know,' said Penna. 'Who are you?'

'Um, Veeka.'

'I'm – er – Penna.'

Suddenly the LOPs' instructions changed. *'Time-to-input!'*

'Surely – that's not right? Is it?' asked Penna.

'Uh, I don't know,' said Veeka.

'It isn't,' said a voice behind them.

'The – others seem to think it is,' said Veeka.

Everyone else was heading for the Instruction Zone's Input Station where the students bought subsidised Inputs, according to their LOPs' Recommended Menus.

'Who are you?' Veeka asked the newcomer, a tall, thin boy.

'Queltus.'

'Time-to-shower! Time-to-input! Time-to-socialise! Time-to-exercise! Time-to-sleep!'

'These LOPs are going crazy. Their timing's all wrong,' said Veeka. 'It's really weird. What shall we do?'

'First thing,' said Penna, 'we've got to shut them up.'

But pressing the emergency red button on the control panel didn't stop her little machine from continuing to gabble out instructions in its tinny voice.

'Time-to … Time-to—'

'Shut up, you stupid thing!' shouted Penna, shaking her wrist.

'That won't help,' said Queltus. 'We need

to dismember them.'

Veeka and Penna looked at him in surprise.

'We don't know how to,' said Penna.

'And if we did,' said Veeka, 'we'd be in real trouble with the Controller of Instruction, dismembering our LOPs in the Instruction Zone.'

'But if we don't do something, we'll be driven mad,' said Penna.

'We could try taking them off,' said Veeka.

'Don't be silly,' said Queltus. 'That's impossible. They've been welded to our wrists since birth.'

'As you're so clever, how do we dismember them then?' Veeka asked. 'We're not supposed to know that yet.'

'Not for another two years, until we get to the Upper Arena,' said Penna, 'and then we have to be assessed for our suitability. Only about five per cent of students actually study Dismemberment.'

'I just happen to know,' said Queltus.

'How?' asked Veeka. 'Anyone who does is supposed to keep it secret. You're making this up.'

'No, I'm not,' said Queltus. 'I do know, and if you've got any sense you'll do exactly as I tell you.'

Chapter Two

The way Queltus spoke was unnerving. But Penna couldn't stand the noise.

'OK,' she said eventually. 'I'll do anything to stop this racket.'

Queltus looked around the Arena; all the other students had gone.

'Right,' he said. 'Now watch and listen.'

The two girls carefully followed his

instructions as he took them through the LOP's Dismembering Sequence.

They each ended up with a pile of minute screws, tiny rolls of metal foil, fine silver wires, miniscule microphones, diminutive printed circuits and microchips. They scooped them up, and put them into their belt-pouches.

'We'll liquidise them later,' said Queltus.

'What do we do now?' asked Penna, realising she'd absolutely no idea without her LOP to prompt her.

'Let's get out of here,' said Queltus.

Veeka and Penna looked at each other.

'Have you got any better ideas?' asked Queltus.

Penna hesitated.

'OK, then,' she said. 'We might as well stick together.'

When they came out of the tunnel from the Instruction Zone the Horizontalator was completely empty.

'Where's everybody gone?' asked Veeka.

Queltus shrugged.

'Where shall we go now?' asked Penna.

'We could go to the Forum,' said Queltus. 'It looks as if something's going on there.'

He pointed to the screen by the Exit. Pictures were flashing up of the Forum, crowded with people. At least she and Veeka wouldn't be on their own with Queltus. There could be safety in numbers.

'OK,' she said. 'Let's go!'

Aboard the Horizontalator they flashed past crowded Input Stations and Leisure Venues.

'Why's everyone there at the same time?' asked Veeka. 'That's not allowed.'

'Something's happened,' said Queltus.

'But what?' asked Penna.

Queltus shrugged again.

The Forum was thronged with people. All the Input Stations were filled with the sound of LOPs chanting *'Time-to-input!'*

At the Leisure Venue people pounded away on Sprinting Simulators, thrashed up and down the pools, heaved weights, threw javelins.

'Time-to-swim … run… Time-to … work-out… Time-to…' The LOPs were giving orders frantically. People were rushing from one activity to another, crashing into each other, jostling for places on the Simulators and in the Pool. It was so different from the usual calm, orderly atmosphere of the Leisure Venue. Normally people moved round in a clockwise direction, from one activity to another, at regular intervals according to prompts from their LOPs. They didn't touch

14

each other, or speak. But today they were shoving, pushing and shouting.

'I don't like this,' said Veeka.

'Why not?' asked Queltus. 'It looks like fun! Everything's usually so *boring*.'

Veeka stared at him. 'Don't be stupid. It's chaos!'

Queltus frowned.

'You haven't told us who showed you how to dismember,' said Penna.

'No one,' said Queltus. 'I found out for myself.'

'I don't believe you.'

'Let's have a Liquid Input, if we can get one,' said Queltus. 'I'll tell you then.'

'Is it time for Input?' asked Veeka.

'If we want it to be,' said Queltus. 'We've dismembered our LOPs, so it's up to us.'

Rather uncertainly Penna and Veeka followed him to a Liquid Input Station.

'I can't remember my Recommended Menu,' said Veeka. 'I don't know the code.'

'It doesn't really matter,' said Queltus. 'Choose whatever you want.'

He chose 129. Penna hesitated, and then pressed number ten. Veeka did the same. They took their containers and found a space to stand near the entrance.

'I discovered the instructions on the NetSphere,' said Queltus. 'I put the word "dismember" into Investigator. I tried it in all the old languages – French, Spanish, Italian, German, Dutch, Portuguese, even that made-up one, Esperanto. Didn't get anywhere. So I went down to Archives to look at the actual books people used, way back, dictionaries of the really dead languages – like Latin. No good. Then I found a Greek dictionary – supposed to be Modern Greek, but it was really old. I found

the Greek word for dismember – diamelizo –
except their alphabet's different. I changed
the Language Setting on my PC to Greek
and then tried again.'

'What happened?' asked Veeka.

'In the end I found the Diamelizo Locus.
I printed off the instructions, learned them
by heart, and then liquidised them.'

'Very clever,' said Veeka.

'Are you being sarcastic?' asked Queltus in
a cold voice.

'No, she's not,' said Penna. 'You *are*
clever.'

Queltus narrowed his eyes.

'Even cleverer than you think,' he said.

Queltus might seem only a gangling boy,
but there was something scary about him. He
knew so much it made Penna feel jumpy.
They should keep on the right side of him.
He'd make a dangerous enemy.

Chapter Three

'Any more Liquid Inputs?' asked Queltus.

'No, thanks,' said Veeka. 'I've had my quota.'

'Doesn't matter,' said Queltus. 'Come on, enjoy yourselves! We're free of our LOPs, for the first time in our lives! Penna?'

'No, I don't want any more.'

As soon as Queltus had gone to get

himself some more Liquid Input, Penna asked, 'What's bothering you, Veeka?'

'Something's not right. He knows a lot more than he's letting on. I don't trust him.'

'Me neither,' said Penna. 'I think he's enjoying all this.'

'I don't know if we could manage without him, though,' said Veeka. 'I'm so used to depending on my LOP.'

'We'd have to decide what to do ourselves, and we're not ready for that yet,' agreed Penna.

'He's coming back. Shall we stay with him for a bit longer?'

'Yeah,' said Penna, 'until we feel a bit more confident. Just make sure neither of us is ever alone with him. Later on, we can say we need to go to the Output Station and get away from him then.'

'He can't come with us there!' laughed

Veeka. 'Sssh! Here he is.'

'What are you laughing at?' asked Queltus.

'Oh, those people over there,' said Penna quickly. 'They're getting into a fight about whose turn it is on that Simulator.'

'Stupid!' said Queltus. 'Can't think for themselves.'

'There are lots of fights going on,' said Veeka. 'It's turning nasty.'

'I fancy some Solid Input now,' said Queltus. 'I'm hungry.'

'Hungry? What's that mean?' asked Veeka.

'Oh, Veeka, don't you know *anything*?' Queltus said impatiently. 'Before LOPs, people ate, you know, inputted, when they were hungry, drank when they were thirsty. But then they started eating when they *weren't* hungry, drinking when they *weren't* thirsty.'

'So what happened then?' asked Veeka.

'Supplies ran out, people got overweight and ill. The Controllers introduced LOPs to instruct people when to eat and drink, and to regulate the amounts allowed. This worked really well so they developed LOPs to control our decision-making about every single thing we do – sleep, leisure, socialising – everything.'

'That seems sensible,' said Veeka.

'Not everybody would agree about that,' said Penna thoughtfully.

'Why ever not?' said Queltus.

'How do you know all this?' asked Penna. 'It's not in any of our Instruction Programmes about the Past.'

'I found out for myself,' said Queltus.

'Again! You think yourself *so* clever,' said Veeka.

Penna was still looking thoughtful. She frowned at Veeka, and shook her head slightly.

'Let's go and get some Solid Input, like you said, Queltus.'

At the Solid Input Station one man dragged another away from a table, while a woman grabbed the Solid Input Box he'd just opened. She stuffed the contents into her mouth.

People queuing at the Dispensing Cabinets snatched Input Boxes from the people in front of them. The Dispensing Cabinet nearest the door had run out of supplies. The people who'd been waiting were fighting among themselves. Others were heading for the door looking ill, clutching their stomachs.

'There's nobody our age or younger here,' said Penna. 'I wonder why?'

'Not part of the plan,' said Queltus.

'What plan?' asked Veeka.

'Oh, nothing – what I mean is – there

wouldn't be any students or pre-students here on a Workday, would there?'

'*We're* here,' said Penna.

'We're not meant to be,' said Queltus.

'We ignored our LOPs,' said Veeka. 'All the others followed theirs to the Input Stations in the Instruction Zone.'

'Maybe the same thing's happening there,' said Penna, looking round at the milling crowds of angry, overfed men and women, pushing, shoving and hitting each other.

'This is gross,' said Veeka. 'I want to go back to my Living Unit.'

'Where's that?' asked Penna.

'Junior Living Unit, Zeeta ONE: 276.'

'I'm Junior Living Unit, Epsilon THIRTY: 945,' said Penna, 'the stop before yours. Let's take the Horizontalator. I just need to go to the Output Station.'

'Oh, so do I,' said Veeka quickly.

'I'll wait for you,' said Queltus.

When they emerged from the Output Station the two girls deliberately went in the opposite direction from where they'd left Queltus, pushing their way through the angry, jostling crowds.

'We'll never get on the Horizontalator,' said Veeka desperately.

Penna realised how much she missed her LOP, but actually it wouldn't have been any use in this situation. LOPs whirred away all around her, issuing instructions nobody could possibly follow – *'Time-to-sleep… Time-to-socialise…'*

She must think for herself!

'If we crouch right down and wriggle through we might be able to make it,' she said.

Veeka nodded.

'I'll go first,' said Penna. 'Hold on to my

belt and don't let go.'

'Made it!' she said, as the Horizontalator
began to move forward.

'I'm really glad to get away from Queltus,'
said Veeka. 'He gives me the creeps.'

'Me, too,' said Penna.

'I wish we hadn't said where our Living
Units are,' said Veeka.

'Try not to worry. Let's hope he won't
remember,' said Penna. 'He's so full of himself
he may not have even heard us.'

Neither of them noticed in the crush that
Queltus was in the next section of the
Horizontalator, only a few metres away,
determined not to let them out of his sight.

Chapter Four

'My stop's next,' said Penna. 'Do you want
to come with me?'

'Yes,' said Veeka. 'I'd feel safer.'

As they transferred to the Verticalator,
the crowd surged forward. The two girls were
swept along, Veeka hanging on to Penna's
belt. Around them LOPs constantly bleeped,
and chanted their instructions.

It was hot and stuffy in the capsule; the air-conditioning wasn't working. Penna felt faint and sick. She moved slightly to get more space so she could breathe. It was then she saw a familiar profile. Queltus!

'We'll get off a floor earlier,' she whispered.

'Why? We can't—' protested Veeka.

'Sssh. Duck down and just do it!'

About twenty other people, all Seniors, got out at Floor TWENTY NINE. Nobody paid any attention to the two girls. Everyone was preoccupied. Intent on following the instructions from their LOPs, they hurried off to the Senior Living Units.

'Why did we get out here?' asked Veeka.

'Queltus was on the Verticalator,' said Penna. 'He's following us.'

'Are you sure?' asked Veeka.

'Definite. I'm certain he didn't see us get out. He probably won't realise straight away that he's missed us. We could wait for the next Verticalator, but it might be ages. Let's take the stairs.'

'They're out of bounds,' said Veeka.

'Come on,' said Penna, 'I'll show you.'

Veeka followed Penna along the corridor, through a door marked NO EXIT, along another corridor, through another door: VERTICALATOR PERSONNEL ONLY, until they reached a third door: DANGER – ENTRY FORBIDDEN.

'We can't go through there,' said Veeka.

'We can. I've done it before,' said Penna.

She tapped seven numbers into the Door Control Programmer; the door opened on to a small landing and a narrow spiral stairway. Absolute silence.

'Come on!'

Penna ran up the stairs, Veeka following close behind. At the next landing Penna tapped in numbers again, the door opened and they went through on to the wide corridor of Floor THIRTY.

Penna aimed her Remote Control at the entrance to Junior Living Unit 945; the door slid open.

'At least it'll be quiet in here,' she said. 'Let's have some nice cold Liquid Input and then decide what to do.'

'So how did you know what to do to get to the stairway?' asked Veeka, putting down her empty Liquid Input container.

'My Grand Senior wrote about it,' said Penna. 'She wrote lots of stuff about the old ways.'

'What do you mean – the old ways?'

'The time before the Metamorf. My Grand Senior and some other female Seniors formed the AMP, the Anti-Metamorf Party – they didn't like the way things were changing. They tried to stop the Metamorf, but there weren't enough of them. The Controllers got into power. So, everything the AMP knew, about life before the Metamorf and the Controllers' plans, they wrote down for their friends and families.'

'Friends and families? What are they?' asked Veeka.

'Before the Metamorf, people made their own decisions, didn't have LOPs telling them what to do every minute of the day. They spent time with people they liked, their friends. They lived in groups called families – Seniors and Juniors together, not separate like us, according to age. Sometimes there were two Seniors, two males or two females, or a male and a female, and mixed Juniors and Middles, brothers and sisters, all living together. Sometimes Grand Seniors as well.'

'Weird,' said Veeka. 'I don't remember any of that.'

'I think it must have been nice,' said Penna. 'But nobody can actually remember, not even Seniors. Somehow the Controllers wiped their memories. All I've got is what my Grand Senior wrote.'

'What happened to her?' asked Veeka.

'She and her friends were arrested and imprisoned,' said Penna, 'and all their Senior family members as well. When they were released their memories were wiped, they were given new identities, and then deported. But they'd managed to record everything they knew, just in case, one day—'

'What?' asked Veeka.

'—someone could do something. So we knew how things used to be, what was good, and what went wrong. They secretly passed these documents on to people who weren't

31

Party members but who believed in the same ideas. And a Senior who knew my Grand Senior made a copy of her notebook, and gave me the original,' Penna paused, 'and that's why I thought – maybe, if we looked at her stuff it might give us a clue about what's happening now.'

'I suppose it might,' said Veeka doubtfully.

At that moment there was a crackling from the Door-Monitor Loudspeaker.

'Penna! Veeka! Let me in.'

Veeka shrank down on to her floor cushion. Penna pointed to the Door-Monitor Microphone in the ceiling. It would pick up their voices, and transmit them to Queltus, waiting just the other side of the door.

Chapter Five

'It's Queltus. Let me in!'

His voice sounded friendly.

Penna flipped open her palm-top.

The words *'Keep quiet!'* appeared on the tiny screen.

Veeka nodded.

'Come on!' called Queltus. 'I know you're in there. We need to stick together. I've got a plan.'

'*U bet!*'

Veeka managed a wry smile.

They both watched the image of Queltus on the Door-Monitor Screen, as he paced back and forth.

'OK, be like that, but you'll soon wish you'd stuck with me.'

His voice was cold and angry, threatening.

After a while Penna pointed to the screen.

'He's gone,' she said. 'We'd better whisper though, in case he sneaks back. I'll show you what my Grand Senior wrote.'

From the back of a shelf she pulled out three flat square containers. In the first two were disks; in the third was a flat block of papers, bound together with rings of wire.

'A real book, with pages you can turn!' said Veeka in awe. 'I've only seen images of books on-screen.'

'Yeah,' said Penna, proudly, 'she wrote the words herself, with a pen. Let's see if we can find anything here to help. I've only looked at the first few pages.'

They bent over the book, studying every page, not sure what they were looking for. They hadn't long. Queltus might come back.

It was getting dark. The automatic lighting hadn't switched on.

'I don't think we're going to find anything,' said Veeka. 'I need a break. My head's throbbing and my neck's so stiff.'

'Stop moaning. We can't give up now,' said Penna. 'Just a few more pages.'

They bent their heads again.

'Look, there!' Penna said.

'It's like notes, as if she was copying something in a hurry,' said Veeka.

'Maybe it was just before she was arrested,' said Penna.

<u>Ten Year Plan</u>

<u>Controllers' Predictions</u>

increase in population growth (people living longer,
decrease in childhood mortality)

decrease in resources eg oil, water, food

<u>Controllers' Proposed Depopulation measures</u>

<u>Phase One</u>

control/ reduce individuals' choices through
installation of Life Organisation Programmes (result:
reduction in food, water, oil consumption, birth
rate; increase in productivity)

<u>Phase Two</u>

artificially create chaos on specified day (to be
decided) by introducing a virus into all systems,
including Life Organisation Programmes (result —
excessive inputting, leading to obesity & health
problems; shortages of food & drink create
tensions; breakdown of heating & air-conditioning
systems exacerbates situation; violence in public
places ultimately leads to dismembering of at least

seventy five per cent of population—

'Dismembering? I thought we dismembered our LOPs?' whispered Veeka.

'I think it means – people—' Penna shuddered '—kill each other.'

Veeka stared at her, horrified.

'There's a bit more,' said Penna, peering at the page.

children & young people (0 to 25 years) especially will be targeted for dismembering. Extra measures will be taken if neces—

The writing stopped.

'That's happening now – Phase Two,' said Penna. 'LOPs going mad, everything breaking down – no auto-lighting, no auto-heating. All those people fighting over Input. But they were all Seniors. Where were the

Juniors? There's just you, me and Queltus. What's happened to the others?'

'What are we going to do?'

'I don't know. We're not used to thinking for ourselves. We've always been told what to do.'

'I wish I could put my LOP back together,' said Veeka, unfastening her pouch.

'No,' said Penna. 'If we hadn't dismembered our LOPs we'd have disappeared like all the other Juniors.'

'Perhaps Queltus is OK after all,' said Veeka slowly. 'It was his idea to dismember our LOPs. Maybe that's what saved us.'

'Yeah,' said Penna, 'but I'm still not sure. He sounded threatening when we didn't open the door.'

'Perhaps he was just annoyed we left him after he'd helped us,' suggested Veeka.

'Maybe,' said Penna. 'I don't know.'

'Shall we copy that last page?' said Veeka.

Penna nodded. She went over to the Copydoc and slid the book into position.

'This isn't working either. I'll just have to tear this page out.'

She tucked the precious sheet of paper safely inside her pouch, and returned the three boxes to their hiding places.

For some time she paced up and down, every so often pausing to check the Door-Monitor Screen. Veeka crouched on her cushion.

At last Penna flopped down beside her.

'Maybe he's gone back to his Living Unit,' she said. 'It's really late. We ought to get some sleep. Let's take it in turns to keep watch.'

'Good idea,' said Veeka, yawning.

'I'll do the first watch,' said Penna.

Chapter Six

It was strange going through the morning routine without prompts from their LOPs, but they managed by reminding each other of what they needed to do.

'That's all taken much longer than usual,' said Penna. 'We need to get a move on and find out what's happening out there.'

'There's nothing on the Door-Monitor,'

said Veeka.

'Off we go then,' said Penna.

'I'm scared,' Veeka said.

'So am I,' said Penna.

'You don't show it.'

'Well, I am.'

'What shall we do now?' asked Veeka.

'I don't know,' snapped Penna. 'You think of something for a change.'

'I'll try,' said Veeka.

Penna was determined she wasn't going to speak first. There was an uncomfortable silence, broken by a familiar voice.

'You were here all the time! Hiding from me, were you?'

Queltus came swaggering along the corridor towards them.

'Humour him,' whispered Penna.

Veeka gave a very slight nod.

'We've not been hiding,' said Penna.

'You didn't open the door. I called and called through your Door-Monitor.'

'It couldn't have been working,' said Veeka. 'Everything's breaking down.'

'What did you want?' asked Penna.

'To show you something,' said Queltus.

'What?' asked Veeka.

'Just come with me.'

'Why?' asked Penna.

'How do we know we can trust you?' asked Veeka.

'It's up to you,' Queltus said. 'But I helped you dismember your LOPs and saved you from what was happening to those stupid people in the Forum.'

'I suppose so,' said Veeka slowly.

'All right,' said Penna. 'But just don't mess us about.'

They took the deserted Verticalator down to the ground floor, and then the

Horizontalator, also empty now, to the Omega stop at the end of the line.

'I've never been as far out as this before,' said Penna.

'Me neither,' said Veeka.

'Then you've not been anywhere yet,' said Queltus.

'I've not missed much,' said Penna, looking around at the bleak landscape.

'It's a pre-Metamorf Industrial Estate,' said Queltus.

'What?' said Veeka.

'A collection of small factories, like Work Units, making things – mostly electronics. That's just a cover now.'

'Cover? For what?' asked Penna.

'Wait and see,' said Queltus, leading them to the back of a shabby single-storey building.

He tapped a series of numbers into a keypad on the wall beside some solid steel double doors. They glided open. The three of them went in, a light came on automatically and then the doors closed behind them.

They were in a huge echoing space, dusty and cold. An ancient rusty pre-Metamorf vehicle was parked at the far end.

'This way,' said Queltus.

In a far corner was a small door, a keypad beside it. Again, Queltus tapped in several numbers before the door opened on to a stairway, narrow and dark. He ran down the stairs, but Penna and Veeka stumbled, feeling their way, holding on to the wall.

When they reached the bottom of the stairs Queltus had already opened the security door; light and warmth flooded out. They entered a corridor, very different from the bleak space above. Gleaming steel walls and ceiling; a constant humming in the background.

After passing several closed steel doors Queltus stopped in front of a door labelled *ODP Monitoring Unit Number 641*. He unfastened a chain from round his neck, flipped open the silver pendant and aimed it at the door.

Inside the room, three of the polished steel walls were covered with monitor screens, but none of them was on.

'Is this it?' asked Penna.

'Yeah,' said Queltus, grinning. 'This is it.'

'Doesn't look anything special to me,' said Veeka.

Queltus frowned. He indicated the sign on the half-open door.

'This is one of the seven hundred rooms with computers monitoring the progress of the ODP. That means Operation Depopulation Programme – the largest scale rationalisation of the world's population *ever*!

Bigger than the three World Wars, all the other little wars, and natural disasters added together.'

'That's nothing to be proud of,' said Veeka.

'It is,' said Queltus. 'It's so logical. It's perfect. It solves all the problems caused by over-population and over-use of the world's resources. Phase One's been very successful, so now Phase Two is being implemented. That's what's been happening since yesterday. The ODP selected Workday 499 as the day to start Phase Two.'

'You're talking like the Controllers,' said Penna.

'You've paid me the greatest compliment ever,' said Queltus. 'It's always been my ambition to be a Controller.'

'Why?' asked Penna.

'Power!' said Queltus. 'Just think! All that

power!'

Penna shivered.

'How do you know about this anyway?' asked Veeka. 'You're only a Junior.'

'But I know *everything* about IT,' said Queltus, indignantly. 'I've been playing around with viruses since I was a pre-Junior. I can hack into any system, anywhere. No Virus Slayer can keep me out.' He laughed. 'I got into the Controlintranet, and found out about the virus they'd created for the Depopulation Programme, and about this place and how to get in.'

He beamed with satisfaction.

Chapter Seven

'So is this virus in the system now?' Penna asked quietly.

'Yeah. It's working brilliantly, isn't it?' replied Queltus. 'Such a simple idea – infecting LOPs first, so people self-destruct, a sort of mass suicide; then infecting all the other systems. Neat, isn't it?'

'It's mass murder,' said Veeka angrily.

'What's the virus called?' asked Penna.

'*Friend of Earth*. Whatever that means. Anyway, it's saving the planet,' said Queltus.

'But it can kill millions of people,' Penna said.

'Ends justify means,' said Queltus. 'Think long-term. That's what Controllers do.'

'You've been brain-washed,' said Veeka.

'Watch it, Veeka,' threatened Queltus. 'You've only survived 'cause I let you.'

'Why did you?' asked Penna.

'Because I decided to,' Queltus laughed.

'But why?'

'Power! Your life in my hands! If I hadn't shown you how to dismember your LOPs you'd have gone the same way as everybody else. Look!'

Smiling, he aimed his pendant. The screens lit up.

'Bangkok, Birmingham, Delhi, Sydney –

New Zealand, South Africa, Mexico—'

As he spoke the screens responded to his voice, displaying images from all the places he mentioned. Close up, or distant, they showed Inputting out of control, people fighting for survival, destroying each other and themselves. Screams, cries of pain and hunger echoed round the room.

Penna glanced at Queltus. There was a look of dismay on his face. But, as soon as he realised she was watching him, he turned away. A moment later his face was expressionless.

'Impressed?' he asked.

'Horrified,' said Penna. 'Those poor people…'

Queltus frowned. It seemed to Penna this was a different sort of frown, not angry or impatient, but worried.

'In the future,' said Queltus, 'it'll be so

much better. The Controllers say—'

'You said you *found* the virus. Since you're so clever can't you get rid of it?' asked Veeka.

'No way,' said Queltus. 'The Controllers—'

'Haven't you a mind of your own?' asked Penna. 'You despise people for depending on their LOPs, but you just parrot what the Controllers say.'

Queltus looked confused.

'I wish I hadn't brought you here,' he said. 'You don't understand.'

'Sorry,' said Penna quickly. 'Actually I do know a little bit,' she continued. 'Not as much as you, of course. I've got something here you might like to see. My Grand Senior knew this was going to happen.'

She delved into her pouch, brought out the carefully folded sheet of paper and handed it to Queltus. He began to read.

' "—*dismembering at least seventy five per*

cent of the population" – Hang on, it was only supposed to be ten per cent—' He looked puzzled. '"—children and young people … especially will be targeted for dismembering—" Why'd they want to do that?' he asked.

'Come on, Queltus,' said Penna. 'Young people use more resources. We're going to live even longer. Of course they want to be rid of us.'

'I don't believe it,' said Queltus. 'I'm sure I got all the info when I hacked into the system.'

'I bet they kept some stuff secret,' said Penna, 'just in case there was a hacker as clever as you.'

'When will the – er – Programme be finished?' asked Veeka.

Queltus pointed his pendant at the blank steel wall. A section of the wall slid back and a monitor, keyboard and chair glided forward. Queltus sat down, and rapidly typed in a series of letters and numbers. A message appeared on the screen.

Latest Information:

Dismembering of LOPs: Result: 85.67%

Dismembering of persons: Result: 11.84%

'Already more people have died than you expected,' said Veeka.

'Queltus, it's a simple choice,' said Penna. 'Leave the Programme to run, and destroy seventy five per cent of the population, including us, or hack into the system again to get rid of the virus, and save lives.'

'If I don't get rid of the virus, I'll die myself,' said Queltus, 'but if I do, the Controllers will find out and dismember me anyway. I can't win.'

'It's up to you,' said Veeka.

'*All* our lives are in your hands,' said Penna.

Chapter Eight

'The virus isn't a Friend of Earth,' said Penna.
'You could be a better friend than that.'

'Don't know,' said Queltus.

'You've been a friend to us,' said Penna.
'Well, sort of – at least some of the time.'

'Friend isn't in the *National Instruction Curriculum*,' said Queltus, 'or the *Metamorf Dictionary of Useful Words & Phrases*.'

'The Controllers don't want people to be friends,' said Penna. 'Lots of words my Grand Senior wrote in her notebook aren't in the Dictionary: *friend, family, community, society.*'

'Can you show us those scenes again,' said Veeka. 'From different places?'

Queltus pointed his pendant at the screens.

'Russia, France, Spain…'

'Go in closer,' said Veeka.

'Moscow, Paris, Madrid…'

'There, bottom left,' said Veeka.

The camera zoomed in. Two women fought over a container. It broke. Water spilled out over the ground. Another woman watched, holding a child in her arms.

'They've just wasted that water,' said Veeka.

'Look at top right,' said Penna.

A boy, carrying an Input Box, was running down a street followed by two young men pointing laser guns at him. A man ran out from a nearby house and threw himself between the boy and the young men. They fired. The man fell to the ground, but the boy ran on, scooped up the box which had rolled into the gutter, and threw it to a smaller boy, standing in an open doorway.

'That man saved the boy's life,' said Penna.

Queltus turned away his head. For a long time he sat at the keyboard, staring into space. Penna and Veeka hardly dared to breathe. Penna could feel her heart thudding, her ears pounding. If only Queltus would say something, do something. But he remained motionless.

At last he looked at the screens again; Penna and Veeka looked too.

They saw people sitting in a circle, passing round a container, each taking just one sip of liquid before handing it to the next person;

people huddling together for warmth in a derelict building; a young woman putting her arm around the shoulders of a frail, old man.

Queltus looked away again. Eventually his fingers began to move, at first slowly, then faster, until they flew over the keys. On the screen icons appeared and disappeared, symbols Penna and Veeka had never seen before, long complicated combinations of numbers and letters, warning messages.

At last he leaned back in his chair.

'I'm going to check the Metamorf News,' he said. 'It's the only way of being sure I've completely deactivated the virus.'

Penna clutched Veeka's hand.

Queltus tapped in the code. The screen went blank for a few moments. The Metamorf Logo appeared on the screen.

'*This is a news flash,*' said the voiceover. '*The Controllers have restored inputting, heating, air-conditioning and lighting systems throughout the World.'*

The screen went blank.

'But the Controllers didn't,' said Veeka. '*Queltus* did, by getting rid of the virus. Why are they saying *they* did?'

'Because they're devious,' said Penna. 'They don't want us to realise they deliberately created a virus to destroy all the systems.'

'So we're all supposed to be grateful to them for saving the world?' asked Veeka.

'Yeah. What do you think, Queltus?'

'You're probably right,' he said slowly.

'But the Controllers know they didn't do it. They'll trace you,' said Penna.

'No. They can't. I've used one of their computers so they'll think it's an inside job. But they'll trace it back to this room, so we've got to get out of here – fast!'

Chapter Nine

As they reached the ground floor they saw
the outer double doors starting to glide open.

'Quick, hide! In here!' whispered Queltus,
darting over to the rusty vehicle.

Crouching down they peered out through
the grubby windscreen. Two female and two
male Seniors came in, walked rapidly over
to the far corner and disappeared through

the doorway.

'Run for it!' said Penna.

They scrambled out and ran.

'Let's go to my Living Unit,' said Penna, once they were on the Horizontalator.

Veeka nodded.

'Queltus?'

'Do you want me to?' he asked, surprised.

'Yeah.'

'OK, thanks.'

As soon as they arrived Penna selected the Information Channel on her wall-screen. It was blank.

'That's weird,' said Penna. 'We saw that news flash in the ODP room.'

'Maybe something else has happened,' said Veeka.

'I'll leave it on,' said Penna, 'so we'll know as soon as it's working again.'

They sat and watched the blank screen.

It seemed to glare back at them. Penna was so tired. She could feel her eyelids closing, her head dropping forward. She forced her eyes open. Suddenly, jagged lights flashed across the screen. There was a jumble of sounds. Then the screen went blank again.

'Oh, no!' said Veeka. 'I thought something was happening then.'

More flashing light, a blur of sound.

'Thi – es – om – ti – pa—'

'This is a Special Announcement from the Anti-Metamorf Party. The AMP has taken control of all News Broadcasting.'

'The AMP!' shouted Penna.

'Sssh!' said Queltus.

'There were extraordinary scenes today when the world-wide LOP system went into over-drive, and completely broke down. Further breakdowns occurred in the inputting, heating, air-conditioning and lighting systems.

'At first there was panic; people were fighting over supplies. But this didn't last long. Filmed reports from around the world show people, LOP-free, beginning to respond in unusual ways, helping each other, sharing resources. Observers are using out-of-date words such as "co-operation"and "friendship" to describe what's happening.

'Sources reveal a virus was deliberately introduced into our systems. The Controllers claimed they were responsible for deactivating this virus. But more recent information confirms it was the Controllers themselves who created the virus, in order to reduce the world population, as part of their Ten-Year Plan. Because they were so sure they had total control they were completely taken by surprise when their plan did not work. Once the virus had been deactivated they were in chaos, and fled to their underground bunker, where they were arrested.

*They have been imprisoned in one of their own
High Security Jails, and will be tried for
attempted genocide.'*

'Your Grand Senior got it right,' said
Veeka.

'Yeah, she did,' said Penna, smiling.

*'Sadly, none of the original members of the
AMP are still alive. But the documents they left
in safe-keeping inspired others to create a world-
wide Resistance movement. When the virus
caused all the systems to break down the
Resistance seized the chance to overthrow the
Controllers' regime and re-establish the AMP.
They have formed an Emergency Committee
until an International Election can be held.*

*'Meanwhile a unanimous decision has been
taken that the LOP system will not be restored.'*

'No more LOPs!' cried Penna joyfully.

*'A statement issued by the Emergency
Committee says: We do not know how the virus*

was deactivated, or by whom. But whoever did
so has saved millions of lives.'

'You've done it, Queltus!' said Veeka.

'Friend of Earth!' said Penna.

Queltus shook his head.

'No, I shouldn't get the credit. I only did it
because you two made me realise the virus
was a terrible thing.'

'Then we did it together,' Veeka said.

'My Grand Senior would have been so
proud of us!' said Penna.